Chomp
Goes to School

BONNEY
PRESS

Published by Bonney Press,
an imprint of Hinkler Books Pty Ltd
45–55 Fairchild Street
Heatherton Victoria 3202 Australia
www.hinkler.com.au

BONNEY
PRESS

Author: Melissa Mattox
Illustrator: Mark Chambers

ISBN: 978 1 4889 2879 6

Printed and bound in China

To my son Eric

Chomp
Goes to School

Written by Melissa Mattox

Illustrated by Mark Chambers

Today was Chomp's first day at school. He was afraid he wouldn't make any new friends. He swam slowly behind his dad towards the coral gates of the school as the other fish darted and splashed out of their way.

"Keep your dorsal fin up and don't forget to smile," said Chomp's dad reassuringly.

Chomp nodded, but he could hear whispers from a passing pod of dolphins. "I hope I'm not in the shark's class," said one.

"There's no way anyone is going to want to sit next to him," hissed another.

Chomp tried to remember what his dad said about smiling, but he knew it wouldn't be easy.

It seemed that everyone already had lots of friends.

Chomp tried to introduce himself to his fellow classmates. He remembered what his father said and did his best smile.

"Hello, I'm..."

...but nobody wanted to talk to him.

At the playground, things didn't get much better.

Chomp tried to join in
with hide and seek.

"...nine, ten.
I'm coming
to get you!"

...but nobody wanted to play.

Everywhere he went, Chomp felt like he didn't belong.

When lunchtime came, Chomp still hadn't made one single friend.

He collected his lunch but noticed something was missing. He swam over to a nearby table.

"AHHHH! Please don't eat us!" screamed the crab.

AHHHH!

"Eat you? I would never eat you!" laughed Chomp.

"I'm a vegetarian! Could you possibly pass the sea salt please?"

After that, the other fish found they had a lot more in common with Chomp than they'd thought.

From then on, things seemed to go much easier!

Chomp and his class went to visit historical sites.

They practised their
fishing-line knots.

And they even played Chomp's favourite game of 'chase'!

By the end of the day, Chomp had made so many friends that by the time his dad showed up, he didn't want to leave.

"Please, can I stay here?" he begged. Chomp's dad laughed.

"Don't worry," said Miss Blowfish. "Tomorrow's lesson is something you can really sink your teeth into."